SERENITY Secrets

SERENITY
Secrets

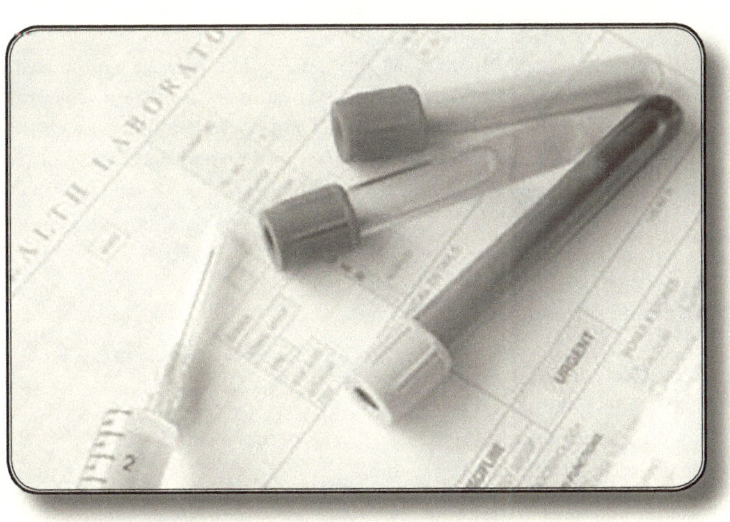

BETTY GOSSELL

Other Books by Betty Gossell

The Boarding Pass (with Karen Pickens) 2018
Future Flights (with Karen Pickens) 2019
A Home For Molly 2019
Wheels Down (with Karen Pickens) 2020
Gate to Gate Trilogy (with Karen Pickens) 2020

DEDICATION

I would like to thank my friends who have been so encouraging during the resurrection of my writing dreams. You mean more to me than I can ever say;

To my co-workers, both past and present – we share a love of medical terminology and all things clinical, and have had some of the most interesting conversations that most people will never understand;

And to my family - your support has been so appreciated. And especially to my daughter Karen, who is my main cheerleader: I could not have done this without you. Thank you so much for all the love and inspiration.

CHAPTER ONE

"I've gone over the test results, and everything looks promising," Dr. Andrea Maddox said to her associate Dr. Jack Tatum. As co-owners and directors of Serenity Springs Memory Care and Hospice, they shared a fairly close bond and friendship. Standing behind her desk, Dr. Tatum leaned across her shoulder and peered eagerly at the stacks of lab reports. His strong aftershave was almost overpowering.

At age 33, Andrea was a fairly new physician. She was quite petite with short black hair and hazel eyes, and her tawny skin was quite typical of her middle-eastern ancestry. Although he was only about fifteen years older than her, she looked up to Dr. Tatum as a mentor and father figure. They had met a few years earlier at a medical conference in Dallas, and she was captivated by his knowledge and charisma. He was quite tall (almost 6'3") with a muscular build and a hint of graying at his temples. His dark brown eyes could appear moody at times, and he commanded respect with his strong personality wherever he went. When he contacted her after the conference with an offer to join him in opening Serenity Springs, she was flattered and wondered why she was the one chosen from such a large group to be his partner. She used the inheritance from her wealthy parents who had been killed in an auto accident as her share of the investment in the new facility. In a very short time, they were well respected throughout the Midwest for their innovative Alzheimer's care. Her background was in research and clinical trials, and she let Dr. Tatum handle the finances and business aspect of the facility. She had little access to the details of the financial records, but trusted him to make those kinds of decisions. They were very different in personality as well – Andrea's office was spotless with all of her files neatly organized and her curtains always wide open so she could admire the flower garden outside. Jack's office, however, was dark and gloomy, with his shades rarely open. Papers were strewn about and books were piled on the chairs. Andrea always dreaded going into his office as it seemed so depressing, in addition to her never being able to locate anything.

"Let me see the results," he said excitedly. After a quick look at the lab results, he gasped. "This is exactly what we were hoping for! What if we increase the dosage? Can we get even better results?"

"It's possible," Andrea said slowly, "but I would hate to overdo it. We can't be sure of toxicity or side effects. I'd really rather take it one step at a time."

"Well, we need to push it anyway. Maranatha is breathing down my neck and wanting answers NOW.

This 'fountain of youth' formula will make us all rich! In the meantime, we have the perfect test subjects – no one will get the least bit suspicious if they die……I mean, that's what a hospice is for, right?"

CHAPTER TWO

Margaret Ramsey pulled her baby blue Chevy Camaro into the parking lot of Serenity Springs. It was a lovely spring afternoon, and she paused a moment to inhale the scent of freshly mowed grass and to hear the sweet sound of birds being carried by the warm breeze. After an especially harsh winter, she was thrilled to finally be able to enjoy being outside. Slightly heavyset with graying brown hair, she looked much like her mother had, although she was much shorter than her mother had been. It was a family joke that someone mixed her up with another baby in the delivery room, since she was by far the shortest one in her extended family. After a few minutes of relaxation, she knew it was time to go inside. Every afternoon she came by after her job as a bank manager to visit her father Theodore. And every day it got harder and harder to go inside, as he recognized her less and less.

Serenity Springs had been such a blessing when it opened two years ago – it was not all that far from her home in Clayton, Missouri, and her father had been getting too difficult for her to manage at home. She had hired a sitter for him during the day, but he was often disoriented and borderline violent. She researched several facilities, but kept coming back to Serenity Springs and its sterling reputation. Located on several acres among gently rolling hills, the environment was appealing and comforting, and it did not feel at all like they were in the city. The day she moved him she felt a sense of relief, but was also filled with sadness, feeling that somehow she had failed him by having to have him admitted to a facility. She thought back to conversations with her mother and father several years ago.

"Margaret, please promise me you will never put me in one of those horrible nursing homes," her mother had pleaded. "They are full of dreary furniture and bad food. I've seen the stories on TV about poor care and the staff stealing from the residents. Promise me, OK?"

"Now Rose, you know she can't promise such a thing. We don't know what the future will hold for any of us. Don't put that kind of pressure on her to promise anything now."

Margaret appreciated her father's understanding. As an only child, the full weight of their senior care would be on her shoulders. Never having married and with no children, she felt very alone thinking about the upcoming future decisions regarding their final days. Money would not be an object in selecting a nice facility, as Theodore had been an electrical engineer and was receiving a nice pension from his old company in addition to his social security and Medicare. Rose was a retired teacher and got a small stipend each month, but that stopped, of course, after she passed away three years ago from breast cancer. She was so brave and never complained, up until the very end when she died at home, Theodore holding her hand.

Margaret signed in at the front desk in the lobby and walked into the day room. Every attempt had been made to make the atmosphere as pleasant as possible – soft muted colors, lots of comfortable chairs, and numerous small areas for reading or playing games. There was a large tropical fish tank along one wall filled with colorful fish. There was none of the stereotypical 'nursing home' feel to the lobby – it was more like a high-class hotel or spa. Relaxing music was playing in the background, but as usual, the TV was blaring an old game show and a couple of the residents were arguing loudly. She found her father in his typical spot at one of the tables working a crossword puzzle. She approached him cautiously, never quite sure what kind of reception she would get. He had not recognized her for several months and sometimes was very suspicious. He seemed taller and thinner than usual, but his sparse gray hair was neatly combed.

"Hi Maggie!" he said as she stood next to him. Maggie – his pet name for her when she was a little girl.

Margaret was startled, not believing he actually recognized her. But his pale blue eyes were clear and he seemed much like his old self.

"How was work today? You still like your job at the bank? No bank robbers today? I heard about one on the news last week. You know, tomorrow would be your mother's 79th birthday. I miss her so much."

Margaret didn't know how to respond – dad hadn't mentioned Mom in at least a year. "I know," she said softly. "I miss her too." She glanced at the crossword puzzle he had been working on, only to see that it was almost done, and done correctly! Usually it was just a jumble of letters that didn't make any sense.

About that time, one of the nurses, Nancy Thompson, stopped by and said, "Good to see you tonight, Margaret. Your dad had a really good day today – his appetite has improved and he even sang in the karaoke contest." Nancy was one of the few friends that Margaret had made over the past year of visiting her father. Dressed in her usual colorful scrubs, Nancy was in her late 50's with a pleasant demeanor, but Margaret knew she could be tough when she needed to be.

"*When Irish eyes are smiling,*" he belted out, "Your mom's favorite song – remember?"

"Yes, Dad, I remember," she said with a question in her eyes as she looked at Nancy.

"Several of the patients had good days today," Nancy commented with a bit of skepticism and surprise. "Maybe it's something in the water."

CHAPTER THREE

Nancy Thompson left the day room and warmed her dinner in the microwave in the staff lounge. It was such a lovely day, and she contemplated taking her dinner outside to the picnic table next to the rose garden. But she decided to stay inside and write a letter to her sister Melissa who was turning 60 next week.

Between bites of spaghetti, she told her sister about the strange happenings at Serenity. It was nothing she could say for certain, just a vague feeling of something being *off.*

After the usual 'happy birthday' teasing her about turning 60, the tone of the letter turned more serious.

"Things at work have been ok, I guess, except I'm a little confused about a few of my patients. There is this sweet guy named Theodore. He's been at Serenity for a couple of years. When he first came in he was fearful and suspicious, sometimes even a little bit aggressive. He has one daughter Margaret who comes in every day. And I mean EVERY day! I think she's only missed three times, and two of them were when we had that horrible ice storm last winter. She's so good to him, and you can tell his disease is breaking her heart. Imagine our surprise when he recognized her today – first time in six months! But it's not just him – there are a few others who seem brighter and more alert. Strange.

"The doctors are about the same – they make such an odd couple! Dr. Maddox is sweet and caring and always seems so interested in the residents, knowing most of them by their first names. Dr. Tatum though – ugh. He is so cold and unapproachable – makes me wonder why he ever became a doctor.

"My dinner break is almost over – hopefully I can get everyone to bed without any arguments tonight! I'll talk to you soon. Love, Nancy."

CHAPTER FOUR

Margaret arrived home from the visit with her father, more confused than ever. What had really happened today? Was he truly getting better? How is that possible? This felt like a cruel trick, and tomorrow he would be back to his pleasantly-confused self, no longer recognizing her or remembering her mother.

She loved the old craftsman-style house that had been her parents' home for almost 30 years. She had moved in shortly after her mother's death once she saw her father's memory start to fade. At first, he had seemed very defiant and resistant to her help, so stubborn and his pride would not allow him to accept her help. But eventually he realized that he was having problems and appreciated having her around.

She reheated some leftovers and sat down in front of the TV. Her old orange tabby cat Barney came down the hall and snuggled next to her. As an only child, she had felt very alone since her mother passed away and her father developed Alzheimer's. Barney was her only companion these days. She fed him a bit of chicken from her dinner and he purred loudly.

Turning on the TV, she surfed around until she found a local news channel. She listened with interest to the end of an investigative report about fraud at the Missouri State Corporate Commission. The reporter, Lacy Mason, had gone undercover to expose corruption that went up to the highest levels of the agency. Margaret admired her bravery and tenacity, plus she was stunningly beautiful. The story ended with her and the District Attorney naming the officials who had been arrested and describing possible prison terms.

She shut off the TV and like most nights, got out her laptop. She continued her research on Alzheimer's patients and looked for advances in treatment, long-term improvement or even a potential cure. Again, she found little hope and was convinced that today was just a fluke – and a painful reminder of the man he would never be again.

Suddenly very tired and discouraged, she turned off the lights and headed upstairs toward her tiny bedroom. Barney trotted ahead of her and took his place at the foot of her bed. Her dad had loved Barney, and the two had been great companions. She would sometimes find Barney sleeping on her father's bed, and it was clear that he missed him. She brushed her teeth and washed her face, feeling the cool water bring relief to her tired eyes. She just had to trust that the staff at Serenity Springs knew what was best for her dad. Opening her bedroom window just a crack, she breathed in the cool night breeze before turning off the light and crawling into bed. She felt Barney move to the crook behind her knees. Normally he wasn't an overly affectionate cat but tonight, especially, she appreciated his closeness.

CHAPTER FIVE

Sergeant Tony Malone closed his laptop and stood up from his desk. It had been another long night at his computer compiling the crime statistics for the quarter, and the sun was just starting to peak over the horizon. How he hated being stuck on this desk job, but it was routine procedure for any officer involved in a shooting to be taken off the street until the case was resolved. Answering phone calls from reporters, doing research – he would be so glad when the investigation was over and he could get back on patrol. This was not his idea of fighting crime! Everyone at the station knew that his use of force had been justified – he just needed to convince Internal Affairs to close the case and let him get back to work. Tony's Italian temperament was a bit too boisterous for an office job. Dark and handsome, he had most of the female investigators swooning, but his heart was elsewhere, although the lucky lady seemed totally unaware.

Just a week ago, he had been one block away from a small regional bank when the call came in that there was a robbery in progress. The teller had pressed the panic button – that was all the information he had as he rushed toward the scene. Just as he was getting out of his car, a witness slipped out the front door and ran to him.

"He says he's got a gun!" the young woman said hurriedly. "There are about five more customers inside, and several employees." She described the suspect as a middle aged white man wearing a St. Louis Cardinals baseball cap, jeans and a black t-shirt.

Tony thanked her for the information and urged her to move across the street to where she would be safe. Pulling out his gun, he called for backup and then walked cautiously toward the bank entrance. Just then, someone matching the suspect's description came running out holding a brown paper bag in his left hand. Tony yelled at him to stop, but the suspect kept running. Tony chased him down the sidewalk, still yelling at him to stop and drop to the ground. Finally the man slowed down, turned around, and put his right hand into his jeans pocket.

Tony yelled, "Keep your hands where I can see them! Get on the ground!" The suspect started to pull something from his pocket, so Tony fired one shot toward him, hitting him just above his left ankle. He fell to the ground, screaming and cursing, and Tony tackled him. A backup car arrived shortly after, and then an ambulance arrived to take the suspect to the hospital.

Everyone at the station seemed to think the incident would be an open-and-shut case, especially after reviewing Tony's body-cam footage. But for whatever reason,

Internal Affairs seemed to be taking a really long time releasing him back to active duty.

Tony looked around the station – always so busy and noisy no matter what time of the day or night. His small desk was near the front reception area, and he was distracted each time the door opened or there was some sort of commotion, which sadly, was way too often. He longed to be back in his own squad car, keeping the community safe.

Finally, his long night was over, and after clocking out he walked across the busy squad room and into a glorious St. Louis sunrise. He climbed into his personal car and headed for home, trying not to think about the job he was missing. Suddenly exhausted, he headed to his condo and hopefully a full day of sleep.

CHAPTER SIX

"**I** thought I told you to increase the dosage," Dr. Tatum said roughly. "Maranatha wants results, and they want them now!"

"I did, but just a small amount," Dr. Maddox answered softly. "It's only been a few days - I don't want to rush this and end up pushing it too far too fast." Standing next to Dr. Tatum in his dark office, she felt the gloomy surroundings matched his mood this afternoon.

"Well, it's obviously working – the first patient is being discharged today. Lois Bancroft – although her symptoms were not all that advanced to start with. I need to see more progress in some of the more advanced cases before I declare our experiment a success."

He paced around the office, his eyes gleaming. "So what if we didn't follow the usual protocols? This new drug will set the medical world on its ear! Keep upping the dosage – I want to tell them the good news by the end of the month."

Andrea walked back to her office and gently closed the door. It was not her place to question Dr. Tatum's authority, but she still felt uneasy increasing the dosage again so soon. Yes, Maranatha wanted to see results, but what was the rush? Andrea wanted the research to be done correctly, and Dr. Tatum seemed all too willing to cut corners and not follow normal protocol. She was worried about the patients – what if this whole thing backfired?

Alone now in his office, Jack Tatum picked up a small trinket box that was half-hidden under some papers and looked at the engraving on the bottom. TJ + YN. Covered in black pearl, it had a delicate gold engraving on the top and sides of a Japanese pagoda. He reached into his desk drawer and rummaged around until he found a small gold key. Inserting the key into the lock on the front of the box, he gently lifted the lid. The box was empty except for a small folded piece of paper and a necklace of silver lotus flowers with tiny diamond centers. His face was clouded with sadness, and then anger. Closing the box, he locked it again and tossed the key back into the drawer. He picked up the box to hurl it across the room, but his mood changed and he set it gently back down amongst the confusion of papers and file folders. The delicacy of the box was in stark contrast to the chaos and disorder of his desk, and his life.

CHAPTER SEVEN

Nancy stood at the nurse's desk, staring at the discharge papers in front of her. In all of her time here at Serenity (and all of the years prior at other hospice facilities) this was the first time she had ever seen discharge paperwork that was not connected to a patient's death. Lois Bancroft went home today! Home! None of her patients ever went HOME! Well, they went to their 'heavenly homes' but that was different.

Lois was a tiny little lady whose symptoms never were very severe. Maybe her doctor had misdiagnosed her, and she never even had Alzheimers. But watching a *living* patient walk out the door made Nancy so very happy, and more than a little suspicious.

CHAPTER EIGHT

Margaret sat across from her father at the puzzle table in the day room. The atmosphere was a 180 degree change from last week. The residents were talking and laughing, carrying on actual conversations with each other. The TV was on but at a normal volume, and no was starting at it blankly as they usually did.

"We had fun today Maggie," her father said. "We went out and fed the ducks, and Norman found a kitten he wanted to keep. Such a cute tuxedo cat – just like one you had when you were little. A really friendly little guy, lots of purring and cuddles. And guess what – Pamela Mitchell got to go home today! She's the third one this week! All of the time I have been here, not one patient has gotten to go home. And this week we had three!"

Margaret looked around the room in disbelief. This was so far from what she expected her father's last days to be like. The whole facility was full of smiling happy patients. There was no one in the world claiming to have a cure for Alzheimer's, but that's what seemed to be happening here. And it was not just one patient who seemed improved, but most of them. Something very odd was happening, and she needed to find out the answer. And she had just the idea of who to ask.

"Dad, I'm sorry, but I need to go downtown for a meeting tomorrow after work and won't be able to stop by and see you. I hate to miss our daily time together, but there is someone I need to see."

"Where downtown?"

"Near the arch on Chouteau."

"Oh, I haven't been to the arch in ages. Remember the first time your mother and I took you? You were so scared – afraid to look out the windows. You sat on the floor in the middle of the observation deck and refused to move. As much as we begged, you wouldn't budge even an inch. I remember when it was time to go, you crawled on the floor toward the little cars that would take us back down. And you whimpered the whole time until we were outside and back on the ground. What a day!"

"Yes, dad, I remember." *I just can't believe you do*, she thought to herself.

Margaret stayed for another hour, talking with him about his day and sharing a few more memories. After their visit was over, she went out to her car and looked up the number for Lacy Mason, the investigative reporter she saw on TV last week. Maybe she could check things out at Serenity? It was another beautiful spring evening and Margaret loved sitting in her car with the windows down, enjoying the fresh air and warm sunshine.

"Ms. Mason, my name is Margaret Ramsey. My father Theodore is a patient at Serenity Springs Memory Care and Hospice. I was hoping I could come and visit with you tomorrow. I can't put my finger on it, but something is just not right there. Please – I really need your help!"

CHAPTER NINE

Lacy hung up the phone and stared at her notes in disbelief. As far as she knew, Serenity Springs had a Five-Star reputation and she had never heard even a whisper of anything unprofessional about them. And who wouldn't want their loved one to get better?

But Lacy understood Margaret's concern, and set an appointment with her for 4:30 the next afternoon. That would give her time for some preliminary research into the facility and its owners. She loved her job as an investigative reporter, and felt an obligation to look into the suspicions Margaret had. She owed it to Margaret, and to her own mother.

She looked at the family pictures she kept on her desk. She didn't have a real office, just a cubicle in a long row of cubicles. The walls were covered with pictures and awards she had won over the years. Soon to turn 40, Lacy bore a striking resemblance to her mother Victoria. Tall and blond, Lacy had often been compared to Princess Diana, except her eyes were a piercing emerald green. Dressed casually in jeans and a blue Channel 11 polo, Lacy leaned back in her chair and pondered the issues that Margaret had mentioned. Was this really a problem that required an investigative reporter? Or was it just concerns of a daughter worried about her father? She was anxious to talk to Lacy tomorrow, but she knew she would be powerless to help unless her boss approved her taking on the assignment.

Looking again at the family pictures, she saw one of her dad and instantly felt a tear spring to her eyes. She missed him so much, and how she could always count on him for objectivity and good advice. What would he tell her to do about this situation at Serenity?

CHAPTER TEN

Tony Malone found himself sitting at his nondescript desk for a second week. Internal Affairs had delayed – again – clearing him from the use of excessive force following the bank robbery last month. He had no idea what was taking so long, but was going crazy being stuck at the desk. He needed to be back on the streets, and soon! There was not much "protect and serve" in the shuffling of papers or running statistics.

He watched with envy as the detectives and other officers brought in suspects, received reports at the start of each shift, and shared the comradery of the street stories. His captain told him today that there would be a continued delay in clearing him to return to active duty since there was no clear-cut evidence to believe that the suspect had been a threat, even though the body-cam footage showed him reaching into his pocket. Once the backup officer had arrived, it was determined that the suspect was not armed and what he was reaching for appeared to be his cellphone.

Tony was frustrated by the way Internal Affairs was treating him, and began pacing back and forth. He belonged out on the street, catching the bad guys, not stuck inside doing paperwork.

Tony's best friend Mario came into station to get ready for his next shift. He stopped by Tony's desk and asked, "Any news?"

"No, nothing. I can't take much more of this, I'm telling you."

"I know, I'm sorry man. At least you aren't out on the street getting shot at every day. Maybe use this time to reconnect with that beautiful girl of yours?"

"Maybe......."

Mario went into the report room and Tony got out his cellphone. Flipping through the pictures, he found one of a tall blond with gorgeous green eyes. She was sitting on a park bench feeding the ducks and laughing. She sun glistened in her hair and she radiated beauty with just a hint of mischief in her eyes. Maybe Mario was right – maybe he should give her a call.

CHAPTER ELEVEN

Margaret was escorted to a conference room at Channel 11 News. Situated on the 20th floor, one long wall of windows offered an inspiring look at downtown St. Louis and the Arch. Another wall was covered with TV monitors, one of them showing what was currently on air. The receptionist had offered her some water or a soft drink, but Margaret was too nervous to drink anything. Maybe she was crazy to be here – maybe she should just go home and enjoy the good days with her father while they lasted. She dreaded the days ahead as she expected him to deteriorate more each day, and eventually succumb to the disease.

After a short wait, Lacy rushed into the room, apologizing for being late. Margaret introduced herself, and then explained about her father's condition and how his Alzheimer's had progressed to a point that he needed to be admitted to Serenity Springs. Each day he had slipped a little further away. She fought back tears as she related how Alzheimer's is called *the long goodbye*, and how she totally understood why. Each day one more small piece of his memory or personality was gone forever.

But then she shared how everything changed a few weeks ago. Her father recognized her for the first time in months, and he remembered her mother and stories from their past. She wanted to be hopeful, but none of her own research had ever even hinted that remission would be possible. As much as she wanted her old father back, she was afraid to be hopeful. And if the difference had been in just her father, it possibly could be explained away. But the improvement seemed to be throughout the facility and patients were even recovered enough to go home. It just seemed very strange to her.

Lacy thought of her own mother, who was in the earliest stages of memory decline. No one had diagnosed Alzheimer's yet, but it was in the back of everyone's mind.

Her mother, Victoria Greenwood, had been the first female prosecutor for the city of St. Louis. She was a throwback to a previous generation – tough, adventurous and fearless. Lacy often compared her to Amelia Earhart for being so strong and breaking gender barriers. So, watching her start to fade was so difficult. Lacy's father Walter had been killed in a small plane crash about ten years ago – a plane that Victoria had been piloting at the time. They had gone from St. Louis to Memphis for a long weekend to celebrate their 50th wedding anniversary. Victoria had been a pilot for several years and never had any sort of problems before. But this time there had been engine failure just outside of West Memphis and the plane went down in an empty cotton field. Victoria had multiple broken bones, but Walter had died instantly of head trauma. Not unexpectedly, Victoria was depressed after weeks in a rehab and then going home to an empty house. The memory issues started not long after that – a name here, a place there – nothing major and certainly logical at the age of almost 80. Lacy had helped her sell the house and move into a smaller apartment, but she seemed a shell of her former self.

Lacy told Margaret that her preliminary research had not turned up anything concerning. There were no violations filed against the facility, but said she would check into it further and get back with her soon, hopefully by the end of the week. Margaret thanked her for the information and promised to keep in touch if anything else happened at Serenity in the meantime.

After Margaret left, Lacy picked up her cell phone and called her old friend Tony Malone. She was surprised that she could still dial his number from memory. Waiting for Tony to answer, she remembered how they first met six years ago on a blind date. She had fallen for him almost immediately and they had dated steadily for several months...she wondered what she had done to cause him to stop calling her.

CHAPTER TWELVE

Tony answered the phone on the third ring. "St. Louis Police Department, Sergeant Malone speaking."

"Hi Tony, this is Lacy. Got time for a few questions?"

"Lacy – can you believe I was just thinking about you? Do I have time for you? Sure! I was about to head out to dinner, but how can I help you?"

"I need you to run a couple of background checks for me on a Dr. Andrea Maddox and Dr. Jack Tatum. Anything you can dig up - legal, financial, you know, the usual stuff we ask for."

"So, what's going on?"

"I'm not really sure just yet. The doctors run a memory care facility called Serenity Springs, and a family member was just here expressing some concerns."

"What kind of concerns?"

"Just some vague irregularities and some suspicions. Not sure if it's anything serious, but I told her I would check."

"Interesting. I'll dig around and see what I can find. I'll let you know what I come up with. It shouldn't take too long."

"Thanks. How much longer are you stuck inside?"

"Hopefully only another week or so. This will help keep me busy until then."

"Good, I know you want back out on the street. Even though I didn't cover the bank robbery for the news, I couldn't believe it when I heard about it. Anyone who knows you knows you would never use force that wasn't called for."

"Thanks, I appreciate the vote of confidence. Hey, how about lunch sometime next week? We could go to that Italian place you love so much in Clayton."

"You mean, the place YOU love so much? The one that reminds you of your Nana?"

"After all these years, you still know me pretty well. Isn't that where we met for our first date?"

"Good memory! I'm always game for some good fettucine, you know that!"

"Ok, I'll do your research, and we'll set a date for next week. Talk to you later, Lacy!"

"Thanks, Tony, I really do appreciate it."

CHAPTER THIRTEEN

Two days later, Dr. Andrea Maddox paged head nurse Nancy Thompson to report to her office as soon as possible. Wearing her favorite Rainbow Brite scrubs, Nancy was curious why she was summoned so urgently.

"I need to make sure you are giving all of the patients these new vitamins. They are purple – not the red ones from last week – ok?" Dr. Maddox said sternly.

"Sure – purple instead of red. What's so special about the new ones?"

Dr. Maddox hesitated a moment and then said, "The formulation is a bit stronger and it might help with both short and long-term memory."

"Maybe I need to take a few – I forgot where I parked my car at the mall last weekend. I can't tell you how long it took me to find it! I wandered around and around – finally had to call a security guard! It sure made me feel foolish."

Dr. Maddox smiled weakly and said, "That will be all, Nancy. Just make sure everyone is taking the new vitamins. Everyone!" and she handed her a bottle of large purple capsules.

"Sure thing," Nancy said as she left the office. She was just trying to make a joke – she just didn't understand why Dr. Maddox always seemed in a bad mood lately.

Andrea looked out the window and watched gathering storm clouds darken the sky. Something felt very wrong – she just did not understand what it was, or how it would be impacting all of their lives very soon.

CHAPTER FOURTEEN

That same afternoon, Lacy called her mother and asked if she could take her out to dinner at her favorite restaurant – Cracker Barrel.

"Any special reason?" Victoria asked. "You sound like you have something on your mind."

"Just a new story I'm working on. I could use your opinion. Is 6:00 ok?"

"Sure, I'll be ready. I think I need some of their yummy dumplings tonight!"

Lacy arrived a few minutes early, fully aware that her mother had probably been ready for a half an hour at least. Lacy was so thankful that her mother could still live alone in her little apartment. She did really well managing things by herself, but Lacy had splurged and hired a housekeeper to come twice a month to do the heavier cleaning, change the sheets, etc. Lacy wondered how much longer she would be safe alone, though. Just last week she had forgotten to turn off the stove and almost caused a fire. Lacy worried about her all the time, and tried to call her at least three times per week. But for now, the best she could do was make sure she was in a gated apartment complex in a low-crime area, and to watch for signs of further decline.

Victoria stepped outside her apartment and walked toward Lacy's bright red Jeep Cherokee. Dressed in a blue pantsuit with a white ruffled blouse, she certainly did not look her age. She easily climbed inside, and Lacy asked the usual questions about turning off the stove and locking the door.

"I remembered, Lacy. I double-checked everything. I know you worry, but the incident last week was just a fluke, I promise."

"I know, mom, but you know I'm just concerned about you."

"I'm fine, really. And I'm so ready for dinner and to hear about your new story."

Seated comfortably in a booth in the back corner, they ordered their dinner and Victoria leaned back in her chair and said, "Ok, spill it. I can tell this story has you pretty upset. You hardly said a word during the drive over here."

"Mom, what do you know about Serenity Springs? Do you have any friends there?"

"Serenity Springs? That new Alzheimer's place? No, I don't think so. Why? What's going on?"

"I'm not sure just yet. If I tell you something, do you promise not to mention it to anyone? Not your bridge group – anyone! It might not be anything at all, but my gut tells me I need to check it out."

"Of course, I promise – talk to me."

Lacy told her about the call from Margaret and her concerns with patients actually getting better instead of regressing further into the disease. Victoria agreed that it certainly did sound odd. She didn't know anyone who ever got better after an Alzheimer's diagnosis.

"I have a contact at the Police Department – you remember Tony? He is doing background checks on the owners, but I wish there was some way to get inside and look around. I was hoping you had a friend there that we could go visit – we could use them as our excuse to see if things are on the up and up."

"But what if you were there to visit me?"

"What? What do you mean?"

"Perhaps I need to become their newest resident. I could observe during the day and you could snoop in the evenings when you visit."

"Mom, that's crazy! First off, you don't have Alzheimer's, so I'm not sure why they would admit you. Second – if something unethical IS happening, it could be way too dangerous! I can't risk anything happening to you just for a story!"

"It's not just for a story - if something is wrong, you owe it to the patients and their families to figure it out. You would want someone to do the same if it was me being harmed."

"You're right, of course. I just don't know how to make it work."

"Why don't we call your cousin Larry? He's a family doctor but maybe he would write the admit order – and he could help keep an eye on me for you."

"I don't know, mom. If anything ever happened to you…."

"I'll be fine, I promise. Let me help with this – please!"

Their dinner arrived, and they discussed the situation further over Victoria's dumplings and Lacy's fried chicken dinner. Lacy promised to contact her cousin Larry if Tony came back with anything suspicious.

"You know, Tony is such a nice guy. What ever happened to you two?"

"Oh, mom…….I'm too old to discuss my love life with you."

"And you are too old to let too many more handsome young men get away! He seemed really sweet on you, and I hate to see you alone all the time."

"I'm just really busy mom, but since you asked, we're having lunch one day next week. Happy?"

"Of course I'm happy Lacy, if you're happy. One of these days I'll be gone, and I want you to have someone and something in your life besides work."

"OK, mom, ok. Let me get you home and I'll talk to you in a few days, ok?"

Lacy drove back to Victoria's apartment in a light rain, and as she was getting out of the Jeep, Victoria said, "I'm serious about helping, Lacy. It's important to me to help if I can."

"I know, mom. I'll let you know what Larry says. Goodnight, mom."

"Goodnight, Lacy. I love you."

"I love you too, mom."

CHAPTER FIFTEEN

"**M**aggie – I'd like you to meet my new friend, Victoria Greenwood. She was just admitted today," Theodore said proudly.

"Hello Ms. Greenwood," Margaret said.

"Call me Victoria, please. I'm a little nervous about being here, but your father has been so nice to me today. At least my daughter Paula will be here later."

"It is a great place," Margaret agreed. "I'm sure everyone here will take great care of you."

Lacy arrived a few minutes later and stopped at the front desk. She signed in using the fake name Paula Greenwood. Wearing glasses instead of her usual contacts and a dark brown wig over her blond curls, she hoped she looked sufficiently different in case someone thought they recognized her from TV. Her cousin Larry was not keen on admitting Victoria to Serenity Springs, but had eventually agreed. He had one other patient there as well who had actually been showing signs of improvement. He found this progress very curious, and he promised to keep an eye on Victoria at the same time.

"This is potentially very dangerous Lacy," he had said when they met last week, "both to you and to your mother. But we know how stubborn your mother can get when she gets an idea in her head. We have all heard stories about Aunt Vickie and her adventures when she was younger. Quite a trailblazer she was in her day! As a physician, I would love to have access to some of the patient files – Alzheimer's improvement is totally unheard of. If there really is a chance for remission, it would be great to see the research! But as her nephew, I can't help but be worried."

They talked for quite a while, with Larry expressing his concerns and Lacy countering with how important this investigation might be. Finally relenting, Larry reluctantly wrote Victoria's admission order.

"Hello, mother," Lacy said to Victoria after finding her in the day room. "Did you have a good day?"

"Oh, yes, I really did. I met some of the nicest people. Especially Mr. Ramsey here."

"Call me Theodore, please," he said, smiling back at her.

Lacy and Margaret exchanged knowing glances. Margaret was nervous about Lacy's decision to go undercover and to admit her own mother as a patient, but Lacy had explained the plan to her over the phone yesterday as their best chance to gather information. Her station manager had approved the assignment, sensing as well that something was out of the ordinary.

"My name is Paula Greenwood," Lacy said, holding out her hand. "Nice to meet both of you."

"You, too. My name is Margaret Ramsey, but my friends call me Maggie."

"Maggie it is then! Mother, let's go for a walk in the flower garden and you can fill me in on your first day."

As they started to leave, Lacy touched Margaret's shoulder. "I'm sure we will be seeing lots of each other."

"I imagine so. Nice to meet you Paula."

"Such nice people," Theodore said as he watched them walk out the patio door.

"Yes, very." Margaret said. "I hope they find something soon," she said mostly under her breath.

"Did you say something about the moon?" he asked, slightly confused.

"Yes, dad, tonight is going to be a full moon." Margaret sighed. As much improvement as he had made the past few weeks, it was still obvious that he was confused and needed the specialized care he was receiving at Serenity. Maybe she shouldn't have called Lacy and gotten her involved. And now her mother was involved, too? *I really hope I did the right thing,*" she thought.

CHAPTER SIXTEEN

Nancy drove from Serenity to her apartment in University City. The heavy rain made the drive slow and stressful, and she passed numerous wrecks along the way. Once finally home, she made a mad dash from the parking lot to the entryway of her building. Soaked despite her umbrella, Nancy trudged up two flights of stairs to her efficiency apartment. Thunder rumbled in the distance as she unlocked her door, relieved to be home before the storm got any worse.

She took a long hot shower and then sat at her kitchen table to go through her mail. Buried under a stack of bills and junk mail was a letter from her sister Melissa.

"Thanks for the birthday wishes," it started. "Turning 60 isn't for sissies! I slipped getting out of the bathtub yesterday and twisted my back. Pretty crazy about your patients at Serenity – I've never heard of anyone ever getting better after Alzheimer's – what do you think is going on?"

Nancy turned on the TV and found her favorite medical mystery show. A husband and wife were slowly being poisoned with arsenic by their ungrateful daughter who wanted to inherit their estate and to cash in their $1 million life insurance. Nancy loved these types of shows and tried to solve the cases before the doctors and police did.

Her thoughts went back to Serenity – you don't suppose someone was trying to poison the residents? Or messing with their medications? Whatever was going on, she knew she needed to keep her eyes and ears open.

CHAPTER SEVENTEEN

Dr. Tatum's face was tight with fear. He was sitting at his desk with Dr. Maddox standing beside him. The voice on the speaker phone was being deadly serious.

"Tatum – what is taking so long?" asked a man with a thick Asian accent. "You promised Alzheimer's remission weeks ago. We need to see some concrete results by the end of the week or we will take our funding elsewhere. Have we made ourselves clear?"

"Yes, very clear. And we are close – really close. We just need a little more time…"

"You've said that for months! Time's up – either give us the formulation or we're done – got it? Do NOT disappoint us. You know the consequences!"

"Yes, of course," he said nervously. "I'll call you by the end of the week."

The phone line went dead. Dr. Tatum turned to Dr. Maddox and said, "I don't care what you have to do – up the dosage so we can declare victory!"

"I've already increased it twice in the past week. I really don't think we can push this any faster. We have no idea if the increase will cause any side effects, or what any long-term ramifications are."

"Did I ask for your opinion?" he yelled angrily. "We have our orders – increase the dosage, starting tomorrow!"

Andrea left his office, and Jack picked up the Japanese trinket box. Holding it in his shaking hands, his eyes became dark and his jaw clenched in anger. How he hated having his past mistakes held over him this way.

CHAPTER EIGHTEEN

The next afternoon, Lacy and her mother were taking their usual walk in the garden, which was their only chance to be alone and for Victoria to report on her observations of the day.

"Today was really weird, Lacy – Dr. Maddox herself supervised the administration of our morning vitamins. And they were different this time – bigger than usual. She looked really nervous while she watched us take them with our breakfast. Then Dr. Tatum – who I've only seen a few times – kept walking around the day room and talking to everyone, almost like he was interviewing us."

"Interviewing you?"

"Yeah, questions like *do you remember what you had for lunch yesterday, or what year were you born?*"

"Wow, that's different. You didn't take the pill, though – did you?"

"No, but it was hard this time – they were really watching. Here it is," she said as she handed Lacy a napkin with a large green pill wrapped inside. "Red, purple, now green – every few days is a different color. Look at how big this one is!"

"Thanks – I'll get this to Larry and have his lab check it out. What about the rest of the day?"

"Not much else was different. Lots of activities in the day room, but probably the worst lunch I have had since I got here. I hope you solve this mystery soon, so I can get out and eat some real food!"

They sat on one of the benches beside the lily pond and talked more about her day. Other than the unusual happenings lately, Lacy could see how Serenity was an excellent Alzheimer's care facility. Even if the patients never did get better (which no one expected them to, honestly), Serenity would be a lovely place for a patient to spend their final days.

After about an hour they went back inside and were met by two gentlemen who were arguing and an older woman in a wheelchair who was yelling at the TV. Across the room she saw Margaret and her father Theodore. He looked almost lifeless, staring out the window. Dr. Maddox was talking to several patients, trying to calm them down. Something odd was happening again, and Lacy knew that time was running out. She needed answers fast!

CHAPTER NINETEEN

D r. Maddox sat alone in her office, trying to make sense of the chaos she had just witnessed. Was the effect of the drug wearing off? Were the larger doses causing side effects? She decided to call to a former Yale classmate, Liz Weaver. They hadn't stayed in touch much since graduation, but Andrea trusted Liz's judgement and medical knowledge.

"Hey Liz, it's Andrea. Andrea Maddox from school. How have you been?"

"Andrea, wow – it's been a long time! I'm good! I started my own private practice a few years ago and we are doing so well we are thinking of expanding. I read about your involvement with Serenity Springs. Hey – ever thought of leaving the world of Hospice care and starting your own practice? Something to think about, you know? You could still focus on the older population, just before they reached the severity that you see them now."

"Ordinarily, I would turn you down flat. I love my job here at Serenity. But lately, well…..some days are harder than others, as you well know."

"Don't I know it! So, what's up? Why the call today?

"I was just curious if you had read anything lately about Cortisol and its effect on the brain? I've been doing a little side research on my own – you know my passion has always been on research rather than direct patient care."

"Cortisol? Can't say that I have. You think it might help with memory issues?"

"Oh, I don't know. I've just been studying its chemical makeup, and wondering if there is potential, maybe something that I should pursue."

"Well, if anyone can find a cure for Alzheimer's, it would be you. I've always been in awe of how your brain can solve even the most complex puzzles. I've gotta run – patients are waiting. Let's do lunch sometime soon, OK?"

"Yes, that would be great. Talk to you soon." Andrea hung up the phone and went back to reviewing the lab reports. She was hoping she had not tipped her hand to Liz about her research – Dr. Tatum would be really angry if he knew. But there had to be something that she was missing.

After about an hour, she got up from her desk and stretched – she stood by her window and looked out into the flower garden. It was so peaceful this afternoon; birds were singing, butterflies were dancing in the sunshine. A few of the patients were wandering among the rose bushes or sitting on a bench by the fountain. Victoria Greenwood and her daughter Paula were seated on a porch swing, rocking slowly and talking. How nice that

Paula came almost every day to visit her mother – so many of the residents had anyone visit at all. She went to the breakroom to fill her coffee cup, and picked up a newspaper that someone had left. She took the paper back to her office and began mindlessly flipping through the pages. She came across a picture of Action News 11's new on-air reporting team. She stared at the picture for several minutes – something looked familiar, but she just couldn't put her finger on it.

Putting the paper aside, she went back to studying the lab reports. But she just could not concentrate. She felt like things were starting to spin out of control.

CHAPTER TWENTY

Tony stared in disbelief at the background report he had just received from his investigator friend Steven Chase. Dr. Jack Tatum had been the subject of numerous ethics complaints for kickbacks at his previous private practice, and had served one year in a minimum security prison for Medicare billing fraud. How in the world had he been able to open Serenity Springs? Where did he get the money? Andrea Maddox had a squeaky clean record – maybe everything was funneling through her? He didn't have all the answers, but knew he had to get ahold of Lacy and let her know what he had found out.

He tried several times to call her, but she didn't answer her phone. Where was she?

CHAPTER TWENTY-ONE

Nancy collapsed onto the sofa in the employee lounge. She had just spent over 45 minutes trying to calm several patients and escort them to their rooms. Dr. Maddox sure seemed upset and worried. Nancy knew that behavior issues were often a big part of Alzheimers, but this seemed quite sudden following the past few weeks of relative calm. She really needed to figure out what was going on.

CHAPTER TWENTY-TWO

A few days later, Margaret tried without success to get her father to eat his dinner, but he kept pushing her hand away.

"Leave me alone!" he growled at her. "Who are you? What do you want from me?"

Tears filled her eyes as she looked around the dining room. Just last week, laughter had filled the air along with pleasant conversation and music. Now it was a sea of yelling and chaos. She spotted Lacy and her mother in the far corner; Victoria was looking very stressed and distressed.

"Lacy, what is happening?" Victoria asked, her eyes darting around the room. "This really frightens me."

"I know, mom. I've got to find a way to get into the patient files – there needs to be some sort of distraction so I can sneak in."

Almost as if on cue, two of the men who had been arguing started throwing food at each other. Nurses and other staff came rushing in, including doctors Maddox and Tatum. Lacy took the opportunity to slip out a side door and made her way to the executive offices. She tried several doors before she found one that was unlocked – a storage room with boxes of old files and extra office supplies. She was about to leave when she spied a box labeled "Maranatha Project." She lifted the lid and started flipping through pages of financial reports and lab results. She didn't understand what she as looking at and knew she was in way over her head medically, so she got out her cell phone to take a few pictures. That's when she noticed she had missed three calls from Tony. She quickly took a few pictures and put the lid back on the box. Tony would have to wait.

Peeking out of the supply room door to be sure the coast was clear, she eased back into the hallway and then returned to the dining room. Doctors Maddox and Tatum were still there, trying to calm the patients down. Things were still quite chaotic, so Lacy quickly walked up to her mother, realizing it was likely that no one had noticed she had been gone.

"I got some stuff I need to follow up on," she said softly. "I've gotta run – see you tomorrow, Mom. Will you be ok?"

"I guess – I think I'll just go to my room and get away from the noise and craziness. Good night Lacy – see you tomorrow."

Dr. Maddox was standing just a few feet away and heard Victoria's comment. *"Lacy?"* she thought. *"I thought her name was Paula. Lacy....where have I seen that name lately? There's something so familiar about her....."*

CHAPTER TWENTY-THREE

Margaret closed her eyes as she leaned back in her car in the Serenity Springs parking lot. The earlier beautiful afternoon was gone, and it had started raining about an hour ago. Now it had turned into a fierce thunderstorm and lightening flashed across the dark sky – it was as black as midnight even though it was only 7 pm. She was hoping that the storm would let up a bit before she headed home.

She hated leaving her father this way. Not only was his memory worse, but he was so much more aggressive than he ever was before. She had never witnessed a near-riot like there was tonight! She had no idea what had set the two men off, but the screaming and flying food was frightening to everyone. It took quite a while for the staff to get everyone calmed down. The two men had to be sedated and helped to their rooms by security. *What was going on? Lacy needs to find some answers fast!* she thought.

CHAPTER TWENTY-FOUR

Dr. Maddox sank into her office chair with a sigh of relief. Finally, all of the patients were calmed down and back in their rooms. Obviously, the massive dose of the vitamin had backfired and caused severe reactions in all of the patients. All of them except for Victoria Greenwood – she wondered why? Was there something special about Victoria? Or were they sure she had taken the pills? The nurses would sometimes just leave the meds on the patient's meal trays, even they had all been instructed to be more observant.

Andrea's gaze fell on the newspaper on her desk. A thought flickered in her eyes, and she quickly flipped through the pages until she found the picture of the Channel 11 news team. In the second row on the far right was a reporter named Lacy Mason. She was very tall and blond – strikingly beautiful and almost regal looking. Dr. Maddox stared at the photo and then remembered Victoria's comment "See you tomorrow Lacy." Is it possible? Was Paula Greenwood really Lacy Mason wearing a wig and glasses? Why? She rushed across the hall to talk to Dr. Tatum.

CHAPTER TWENTY-FIVE

After leaving her cousin Larry's office, Lacy went home to figure out her next steps. He had called her earlier in the day and asked her to stop by after her visit with Victoria. Once she arrived, he told her that he had never heard of the Maranatha Project, and the reports she had seen were lab tests that look specifically at brain chemistry.

Lacy lived in an upscale apartment on the 45th floor with a wall of windows overlooking the city skyline. She loved to sit in the dark and look at the sea of lights below her. Tonight's thunderstorm was fascinating with lightening flashing near the Arch, the thunder booming so close she could feel her building vibrate.

Growing up, Lacy had always had a pet of some sort. When they lived in the suburbs, they had quite a menagerie of cats, dogs and even a rabbit. Her hectic schedule now really prevented her from having a pet, but a few weeks ago she caved in and got a beautiful burgundy beta fish she named Sammy. She gave him a little dinner and watched as he puffed himself up in front of a mirror Lacy held up for him. As much as Lacy loved her posh apartment with its modern furniture and clean lines, she did miss the sound of a dog running down the hall to greet her. Maybe someday.

She finally called Tony back and he relayed the information he had found about Dr. Tatum and the Medicare fraud.

"Medicare fraud? Prison? What is he doing running a Hospice facility?"

"I have no idea, Lacy. I'll keep digging – I can see why that family member got suspicious. Dr. Tatum certainly seems like he has lots to hide."

Lacy wasn't sure how all the pieces fit together, but she knew something was very wrong. And she had the gut feeling that all of the patients were in danger, including her own mother.

Settling into her recliner with a glass of wine, she watched the lightening streak across the sky. Closing her eyes, she tried to make sense of all she had seen today, but the pieces just wouldn't fit. What was she still missing?

CHAPTER TWENTY-SIX

"Jack, I think we have a problem," Andrea said timidly from the doorway of his office.

"I know. That scene in the dining hall was a disaster." Jack Tatum was sitting in the darkened room, his head in his hands.

"No… I mean, yes, it was, but there's something else." She handed him the photo from the newspaper and told him about Victoria's slip of the tongue.

"Lacy Mason – here? All this time? Are you sure?"

"I mean, I really do think that it's her. Add glasses and a brown wig? Look closely at the picture!"

"Oh, this is trouble! Big trouble!"

"And another thing," Andrea continued. "Everyone had a bad reaction to the larger vitamin dosage today – everyone except Victoria Greenwood."

"Victoria? Paula's …. I mean Lacy's mother? Then they must know something is going on. Lacy probably told her not to take the pills."

"What are we going to do?" Andrea asked nervously. "I don't want to go to jail."

"No one is going to jail – I'll see to that."

"How? What are you going to do?"

"Just leave it to me. I'll find a way to keep them quiet – both of them."

After Andrea left, Jack paced around his office, hearing the storm rage outside. He opened his blinds just enough to see hail starting to pound on the roses in the garden. Frustrated, he turned his back to the window and then dug around on his desk to find the trinket box. He cupped it softly in his hands as if to comfort himself, then placed it on a bookshelf, half-hidden behind his medical diploma. A pretty fitting place for it, he figured.

CHAPTER TWENTY-SEVEN

Lacy's cousin Larry called just after she got home the next evening. He had studied the pictures Lacy had taken and could not really find anything out of the ordinary – for normal healthy adults, at least. He would have expected a few abnormalities with Alzheimer's patients, though. But what he really wanted to discuss was the toxicology report of the pill she had asked him to test.

"What is it?" Lacy asked. "Why are they being so insistent that everyone take this special vitamin?"

"When you signed Victoria's admission papers, was anything said about her taking part in a clinical trial or experimental treatment?"

"No, absolutely not! What's going on? You're starting to scare me."

"I had a second lab look at the pill – it doesn't match any known formulation on the market today. While is it mostly a massive dosage of a multi-vitamin, it also contains an unbelievably high level of Cortisol, which is a brain hormone. I've never seen anything like it! If I didn't know better, I would think someone was experimenting on the patients!"

"Do you think that is what the Maranatha Project is? Secret Alzheimer's research using hospice patients as Guinea pigs?"

"It's starting to look that way, I'm afraid."

"We've got to find out for sure and get the patients out of there! What do you know about Cortisol – is it dangerous?"

"Normally, no, but I don't think anyone ever studied it at this high dosage."

After discussing the lab results a bit more and today's strange events, Lacy hung up the phone and paced around her apartment. How was she going to know if something illegal was really going on? She got out her laptop and did some additional research on Cortisol. She didn't find anything that suggested it could be added to a multi-vitamin to be given to Alzheimer's patients. Was some sort of unauthorized experimentation really going on? Lacy finally went to bed but tossed and turned most of the night. The few dreams she did have contained a menacing man with dark eyes, threatening to hurt her mother.

CHAPTER TWENTY-EIGHT

Sitting on a wooden bench, Margaret watched the ducks floating smoothly across the pond of the local park, their reflection tinted pink by some of the final rays of sunshine. Last night's thunderstorm had washed the air clean, and she inhaled the fresh scent of springtime. She closed her eyes and let the warm breeze bathe her frazzled emotions. She had just finished another visit with her father. Well, visit was not the right word, since he refused to talk to her. He yelled every time she went near him and swatted her hand away when she touched his shoulder. In fact, all he did was yell or stare out the window mumbling over and over "No more vitamins – stop making me do it!"

Margaret had no idea what he was talking about. She just knew the father she loved was fading further and further away.

"Please Lacy," she said softly. "Please hurry – I don't think he has much time left."

CHAPTER TWENTY-NINE

Dr. Maddox paced back and forth in Dr. Tatum's office. "What are we going to do? She was here again today. I'm more convinced than ever that Paula is really Lacy. She and her mother go out to the rose garden every afternoon – I used to think it was so sweet the way they spend their time together, but now I think it's when Victoria gives Lacy a daily update."

"I think I figured out a way to eliminate the old lady, but someone as high profile as Lacy could be a bit tricky."

"Oh, Jack – eliminate? Is that really necessary?"

"If we want to stay out of jail it is! Thursday is the quarterly open house and tea party. I think it could be arranged for Victoria to get a "special" cup of tea, laced with Nifedipine. A heart attack in an old lady on hospice won't raise an eyebrow. Probably won't even do an autopsy. But as for Lacy….we need to find a different way to make her disappear."

"Nifedipine would be pretty dangerous for her, given her history of hypertension and coronary artery disease as well."

"Exactly."

"They seem to spend an awful lot of time with the Ramseys – Theodore and his daughter Margaret. Do you think they are involved in this whole mess, too?"

"Let's hope not. Killing off one of my patients is bad enough – two at the same time would raise suspicions too much."

"Surely there is another way! I can't believe you would consider KILLING one of our patients! We took an oath to 'do no harm!' Please don't do this!"

Andrea turned to leave his office, and she noticed a beautiful black box on the bookshelf – had that been there all this time? She had never noticed it before.

"Jack, what is that black box? It's beautiful!"

"Oh, just a gift from many years ago. Nothing special."

"Nothing special? It looks expensive, with Japanese carvings on it. Where did you get it?" She started to pick it up off the shelf but Jack interrupted her.

"Don't touch it!" he snapped at her. "Yes, it's expensive. Yes, it was a gift. Now get out of here while I try to solve our problem!"

Andrea slinked out the door, hurt by his hateful tone and tears stinging her eyes. The stress of the Maranatha Project was starting to get to both of them. Oh please let him not hurt our patients, she prayed.

CHAPTER THIRTY

Nancy left the medication room and almost bumped into Dr. Maddox who was standing the hallway, looking like she was about to cry.

"Oh, I'm sorry Doctor," Nancy stammered. "Are you ok?"

"Yes, I'm fine. Just a stressful few days lately. I'm so worried………" and her voice trailed off.

"I'm worried too," Nancy agreed. "These aggressive outbursts are getting out of hand!"

"Yes, they are," Andrea said, although she was thinking more about Dr. Tatum and their potential jail sentences than the patients.

Nancy watched as Dr. Maddox went into her office and gently shut the door. Whatever was going on was really effecting all of them.

CHAPTER THIRTY-ONE

Sitting in her cubicle at the TV station, Lacy spread out her notes and tried to make sense of it all. Covering her desk were random scraps of paper – notes from Margaret's initial call about Theodore; Tony's research; the toxicology report from her mother's pills; the lab reports; the patients who improved and were discharged; the sudden relapse of symptoms and violent outbursts; the doctors' strange behavior; the ever-changing size of the vitamins.

She tried to find a pattern – a common denominator. And what was the Maranatha Project? How does that factor in, if at all? Was something sinister going on, or was it all just coincidences?

"I'm going to sit here until I figure this out – I have to!"

Her cell phone rang, and she saw it was Tony. Maybe he could help her make sense of it all.

"Hey Lacy – hate to bother you but I just learned something, and I knew I needed to tell you as soon as I could. I have a friend in the cyber-security division who owed me a favor, so I asked him to double-check both Jack Tatum and the Maranatha Project. Are you sitting down?"

"Of course – what did you find out?"

"Jack Tatum is not his real name – he was born Timothy Jackson. He changed his name when he went to medical school."

"Changed his name? Why?"

"Turns out he had quite a jouvie rap sheet, including assault."

"Assault? My mother is in that place! How in the world was he able to go to medical school? To open Serenity Springs?"

"I'm not sure about medical school, but it looks like everything is flowing through the other doctor's Tax ID. She has no sort of history other than graduating with honors from Yale Medical School. I would venture a guess that she has no idea about his past."

"What about Maranatha?"

"That was a little trickier for my friend to uncover. The only thing he found so far is an offshore bank account with over $450 million in deposits."

"$450 million? Wow! Anything else? Any idea who is behind it?"

"No idea, other than it appears to originating in Japan. But there have been several wire transfers out over the past six months – and you will never guess who to! To someone named T. Jackson."

"T. Jackson? Timothy? Dr. Tatum? How much are the transfers?"

"There have been four - $1 million each."

"Why would they be giving him money? And does this have any relationship to his work at Serenity Springs?"

"I can't say for sure, but it's sure looking suspicious. And potentially dangerous. Good luck Lacy – I'll let you know if I hear anything else."

Lacy hung up the phone and stared with dismay – and now with fear – at the papers spread out before her. "Think Lacy, think! Why would Tatum be taking payments from Maranatha? And what does that have to do with the patients at Serenity Springs? Is everyone in danger?"

CHAPTER THIRTY-TWO

Three days later, the morning of the Open House, Nancy Thompson was walking down the hall toward the file room when she heard angry voices coming from Dr. Tatum's office.

"Surely, there is another way to solve this, Jack – must we be so drastic?" Andrea pleaded. "She is such a sweet lady! Don't do this – please!"

"It has to be done, and done today! Is everything ready for the open house?"

"Yes, I think so. The dining hall is decorated and catering has everything prepped and organized."

"What about the tea? You know what to do?"

"Yes, I just wish there was another way. I haven't slept in days, worried about this."

"Well, there isn't, so go get everything ready. Don't mess this up!"

Nancy ducked around a corner as Andrea came out of Dr. Tatum's office. Unlocking the drug closet and stepping quickly inside, Andrea softly pulled the door shut behind her. Nancy quietly opened the door and watched Andrea slip a bottle of Nifedipine into her pocket.

"What are you doing with that?" Nancy asked accusingly. "Nifedipine? That's a pretty dangerous heart drug......who are you getting that for?"

"Nancy, just back away and shut the door. Forget you ever saw me – please!"

'Absolutely not! Something strange is going on here – and has been for weeks. I demand to know the truth!"

"Nancy, please – I beg you! Just shut the door and go back to work!"

"Not until you tell me why you have a bottle of drugs in your pocket!"

"That's the wrong answer, Nancy," Dr. Tatum whispered in a low sinister voice from right behind her. "And now you are going to have to pay for being such a snoop!"

He shoved her deeper into the drug closet and firmly pulled the door shut. "You just had to stick your nose into things you don't need to know about." Dr. Tatum's eyes were glaring at her menacingly. He rummaged around on the shelf until he found a syringe and a bottle of Propofol. "Well, your snooping days are over, I'm afraid. Hold her, Andrea!" he demanded while he opened the bottle. Both Nancy and Andrea watched in horror as he completely filled the syringe with the deadly drug.

"Please, no......" Andrea whimpered. "Jack – this has to stop! Not Propofol!"

Dr. Tatum grabbed Nancy's arm and shoved the needle deep into the flesh near her right shoulder. He watched as Nancy's eyes registered fear at what was happening to her. Within a second or two, though, it was over, and she slumped to the floor. Jack used his foot to kick her into the corner of the closet and slid a stack of empty boxes in front of her. "We'll have to leave her here for now. Get back to the party and handle things with Victoria. I've come up with a plan for Lacy. Andrea – focus! We are so close – we can't lose everything now. And you don't want to end up like Nancy, do you?" he said threateningly. Dr. Tatum put another syringe and the Propofol bottle into his lab coat pocket and walked away.

With one of Nancy's shoes barely peeking out from behind the stack of boxes, Andrea was shaking as she locked the drug closet and made her way to the dining room. This whole situation felt so unreal. Did she even know Jack at all? And what was he going to do to Lacy?

CHAPTER THIRTY-THREE

Leaning back into his booth seat at Manzetti's, Tony glanced around the half-empty restaurant. Even off duty, it was hard for him to totally relax and not feel like he had to continually scan the crowd. His captain had just called him and told him to expect a final verdict from Internal Affairs this afternoon. If all went well, he would be back on the street the next week.

He glanced at his watch and noticed it was just now 12:30, the time Lacy had agreed to meet him. He had learned through past experiences that being on time was not always possible for her, knowing the nature of her job. And his – how many times in the past had one of them been really late, or had the date been cancelled altogether? Their waitress stopped by for drink orders, and Tony asked for just water for now. She left a basket of wonderful-smelling breadsticks, but he resisted the urge to sample one early. After a few minutes he heard a familiar voice near the front door and he looked up to see the hostess pointing toward him. Lacy looked so beautiful standing there – Tony wondered again what had gone wrong and why they had quit seeing each other. Sure, they both had crazy-busy schedules, but that shouldn't stop them from trying again, should it?

Tony stood as Lacy approached the table, and marveled at the grace with which she moved. She certainly commanded attention in whatever room she entered, and yet she seemed totally oblivious to how beautiful she really was, which made her even more attractive, if that was possible.

Tony had tried to look nice, without it looking like he was trying too hard. His bright blue polo shirt contrasted with his olive skin, and his khakis were neatly pressed. He had on a bit of her favorite aftershave and wondered if she would remember. They were about the same height, and he looked fondly into her green eyes.

"I'm so glad you are here," he said, "that we are here. You look lovely, by the way."

"Oh, Tony, thanks. You look pretty good yourself. Mmmm, that scent seems familiar."

"Well, it's either me, or the breadsticks. It was hard for me to wait."

"I'm glad you did! I'm starving by the way. I haven't been here in ages but the place looks just the same."

Their server stopped by to ask again about their drinks. Lacy debated for a minute about ordering a glass of her favorite white wine, but figured she shouldn't since it was the middle of the day and she had the Open House at Serenity to go to later.

"Well, I already know I want the fettuccine," Lacy said. "What about you?"

"I think it will be manicotti for me this time. Not my Nana's, but pretty close."

After the waitress left with their orders, Lacy leaned back and closed her eyes. "Let's make a vow not to talk about work today – either of us. At least, not until dessert, ok?"

"I don't have much to talk about, not now anyway. But hopefully this afternoon I will."

"Finally word from Internal Affairs?" Lacy said, sitting up straight. "Great! Everyone knows you wouldn't use excessive force, and the suspect was reaching for something. He had already threatened that he had a gun – what were you supposed to do? Just stand there and let him shoot you?"

"Let's just hope IA agrees with you!"

Their salads arrived, along with a second basket of bread sticks. Lacy knew she would probably regret having such a big meal in the middle of the day, but it had been so long since she and Tony had been here – so long since she had a date, period. Tony was such a sweet guy – how is it that they had stopped seeing each other?

After a few minutes of light conversation, their lunch arrived and Lacy's eyes feasted on the huge bowl of pasta set before her. Oh, she was going to pay for this later by some extra time on the treadmill. She twisted a heaping serving of pasta around her fork and glanced at Tony, who was tasting his first bite of manicotti. "Thanks for suggesting this, Tony," Lacy said as she slid the gooey pasta into her mouth. "Mmmmm."

Their conversation continued light and easy, neither of them talking about work or Serenity Springs. She felt so comfortable with him – how nice it was to have casual adult conversation for a change! Sammy her Beta fish sure was not much of a conversationalist.

Their waitress stopped by to see if either of them would be interested in dessert. Lacy rolled her eyes and asked for a box instead – she still had about half of her fettuccini left and figured she could reheat it later after the Open House. Tony finished his manicotti, but just barely, and said he needed to go home and take a nap. Lacy laughed at him, saying he might sleep through the call from his captain. "Oh, forgot about that," Tony said with a grin. "Guess I had better find a way to stay awake. Maybe I should go to the gym instead."

"I was just thinking the same thing. Gotta keep my girlish figure for TV, you know."

"There is nothing wrong with your figure – nothing at all!" Tony said with admiration in his eyes.

"You sure are good for my ego – I think I need to keep you around."

"That would be fine with me, Lacy. Maybe we can do this again sometime soon?"

"I'd like that. Let's wait until you hear from IA and find out what your schedule is, then we'll work something out. I hate to rush, but it's about time for me to head over to the Open House."

They walked together to Lacy's Jeep, and Tony held the door open as she started to climb in. She paused a moment, putting a hand on his arm and then placed a soft kiss on his cheek. "Thanks for lunch, Tony. See you soon," and he watched her drive away.

CHAPTER THIRTY-FOUR

Margaret arrived at Serenity Springs a little early for the open house. She felt guilty for dreading this afternoon with her father and the other patients, but she knew it was her duty to be there as much as she could, even if he never recognized her anymore.

She entered the room to find Victoria sitting with her father, attempting to have a conversation with him.

"Hello Victoria. How are you today?"

"OK, I guess. Just kinda nervous – not really sure why. Have you heard anything from Lacy lately? She hasn't called me yet today."

"Sorry, I haven't. But I think she planned to be here later, right?"

"I believe so. Oh, there is Dr. Maddox. She seems really uptight lately. She's been watching me like a hawk to see if I take all of my medicine."

Dr. Maddox approached the threesome. "How are you this afternoon?" she asked nervously. "So glad you could come today Margaret. Victoria, is you daughter planning to come also?"

"Yes, she will be here soon, I'm sure."

"Well, enjoy the refreshments. There will be a big announcement in a few minutes, and then some music and cake and ice cream later."

Margaret watched Dr. Maddox walk to the other side of the room and lean against the wall. She seemed really odd today – almost like she was afraid of something, or someone. Margaret hoped that Lacy would get there soon to give them all some answers.

CHAPTER THIRTY-FIVE

Dr. Tatum was about to leave his office to go to the open house when his phone rang.

"Tatum – we have a problem. Or shall I say YOU have a problem. Someone from the US has been poking around in our finances and learned about our wire transfers to you. Do you know who, or why?

"I have a pretty good idea. It will be dealt with today."

"It better be. We have totally run out of patience with you. And you know what comes next, right?"

"Don't worry, I'll handle it."

Jack looked at the black trinket box on the shelf. He took it down gently and caressed it with his large hands. He found the key again, and opened the box but this time he unfolded the letter. Memories of his high school days came flooding back – memories of young love, of the mixing of their cultures, and then the ultimate memory of deception and heartbreak. The box had been her first gift to him, and he gave her the necklace for her first American Christmas. She was a lovely girl, and had attracted a lot of attention from many of the high school boys. He had never intended to hurt either of them, but when he caught her on a date with another boy from their class, he had just snapped, and ended up beating both of them badly. The couple had ended up in the hospital, and Jack wound up in Juvie for a few months facing assault charges. The necklace was returned to him by her family, along with the love letter he had written to her. Little did he know that more serious criminal charges would have been better than the years of reparation he was forced into by her brothers. Changing his name, going to medical school and then being indentured to her family - that may have kept him out of a longer prison sentence, but he was in over his head now – and had been for years – with no way out. And he felt the walls closing in around him.

CHAPTER THIRTY-SIX

Tony paced around his kitchen, his hands trembling as he dialed Lacy's number. He needed to get in touch with her as soon as possible.

Finally Lacy answered. "Sorry, Tony, I was on a conference call with my boss and some studio executives. What's up? News from Internal Affairs?"

"No, this is important! Lacy you have got to get to Serenity Springs right away and get your mother out of there. I'll meet you there as soon as I can. You won't believe this! One of my PI's called me shortly after I got home from our lunch date. He had done some more digging and found out that Maranatha is headed up by two brothers from Japan – Yute and Ryuse Nakamura. They have a much younger half-sister named Yuri who was a high school foreign exchange student 25 years or so ago. When she was in the US she dated a young man named Timothy Jackson – yes, our Timothy Jackson! Timothy and Yuri were a pretty serious couple, but they had some sort of falling out and he was accused of assaulting her and a male student. He spent six months in a Juvie facility – it would have been more but her brothers agreed to not press additional charges. The Nakamura brothers are from a very wealthy family and it seems they bribed Timothy to change his name and go to medical school in exchange for no further charges or Japanese retribution, which would have been very serious by their cultural standards. The feeling is that he would 'owe' them something in return for their silence."

"Assaulting two people? So there really is a relationship between Dr. Tatum and the Nakamuras?"

"And that's not all. The brothers have been bragging that their 'private research team' is on the verge of announcing an anti-aging breakthrough, including a cure for Alzheimers!"

"So it DOES all fit together! I knew it! I'm on my way there right now – the open house is this afternoon with supposedly a big announcement. I guess we now know what that will be!"

"I'll meet you there - be careful Lacy. Tatum has already proven himself to be a pretty nasty guy, even from a very young age."

Lacy sent her mother a quick text as she ran out the door. *"Mom – on my way. Urgent – be very alert! Stay with Margaret and Theodore – don't be alone with anyone else, ok? Just wait for me!"*

Praying for all green lights, Lacy drove frantically toward Serenity Springs. She had a really bad feeling about all of this.

Inside the Serenity Springs dining room, Victoria's cell phone was in her purse, set on the silent mode. She never noticed it vibrating while she was eating a piece of carrot cake, talking with Margaret and Theodore, and wondering when Lacy would arrive.

CHAPTER THIRTY-SEVEN

Lacy slid her Jeep into the first parking spot she could find and quickly pulled on her wig, but didn't take the time to remove her contacts and put on her glasses. She rushed into Serenity Springs and signed in as Paula as she usually did. As she was about to open the dining room door, she looked through the window and saw Dr. Maddox drop something into a teacup and then hand the cup to her mother. Lacy had just put her hand on the door to open it when she heard a deep voice behind her.

"How nice of you to join us this afternoon Paula – or should I say Lacy?" and with a swift tug Dr. Tatum pulled the wig off of her head. "Just what is the purpose of this disguise?"

"Why don't you start by answering some questions for me – beginning with changing your name and using my mother and the others as your unsuspecting test subjects?" She was trying to keep a wary eye on her mother, praying she wouldn't drink from the cup Dr. Maddox had given her.

Dr. Tatum grabbed her arm and started to pull her away from the door. "You think you are so smart. But the game is over, and you are coming with me!" He slid his free hand into his lab coat pocket and was reassured to feel the bottle of Propofol and the syringe still there.

"I'm not going anywhere with you! Let go of me!" Lacy hissed back at him.

"You don't have a say in this, I'm afraid," he said as his fingernails dug painfully into her arm. "Now! Move!"

Just then a blood-curdling scream came from the direction of the drug closet. Dr. Tatum loosened his grip just enough for Lacy to break free and run to her mother's side as she held the teacup up to her lips.

"Mom, stop! Put the drink down and come with me – now!"

Victoria looked at Lacy with confusion, but then set the untouched cup of tea on the table and followed her out into the hallway. Dr. Tatum was nowhere to be seen. Before any explanations could be made, Lacy ran around the corner and pulled the fire alarm. A security guard came rushing toward them and Lacy yelled "Follow me!" as she went running down the hall toward the executive offices.

They were met by a crowd of staff members who were gathered around Nancy's lifeless body in the drug closet. Pausing for only a moment, Lacy rushed toward the file room but she asked the security guard to stay behind with Nancy and also to call the police. She ran to the file room to see Dr. Tatum on his knees in front of the Maranatha Project box, attempting to destroy as many documents as possible. When he saw Lacy, he stood up and reached into his pocket for the syringe and the Propofol.

"We were so close and you have ruined everything!" he snarled at her as he pulled the cap off of the syringe and filled it with the milky white drug. Lacy's eyes filled with fear – she knew what Propofol was thanks to all the media attention in the past few years, and she looked around frantically for a way of escape. She was shocked to realize that Dr. Tatum was actually preparing to jam the needle into himself instead of into her. Lacy stared in horror as he positioned the needle next to his left thigh, but she was suddenly shoved aside by Tony, who wrestled the syringe away from Dr. Tatum.

"You're not taking the easy way out, Timothy Jackson!" Tony said as he quickly put handcuffs on him. "Timothy Jackson, aka Jack Tatum, I am placing you under arrest," and he started to read him his Miranda rights. Dr. Tatum tried to twist his arms out of the cuffs, but Tony was too strong for him.

"Lacy, what in the world is going on?" Victoria asked fearfully, standing behind her in the hallway. "Why is Tony arresting Dr. Tatum?"

"Please go back to the dining room, mom, and I'll tell you all about it in a few minutes. First I need to find Dr. Maddox. But don't eat or drink anything else, please!"

"I'm right here," Andrea said softly from an alcove in the hallway. "I'll tell you whatever you want to know. I'm so sorry……I was just trying to help…."

CHAPTER THIRTY-EIGHT

Lacy and Tony were seated across the picnic table from Margaret and Theodore in the Serenity Secrets rose garden. They were enjoying glasses of lemonade on a warm autumn afternoon.

"So, how do you like the new management here?" Lacy asked Margaret.

"They are really great. It's been six months now since everything happened – we can't thank you enough for all that you did for us and all of the patients. I shudder to think about what would have happened if you two hadn't stopped Dr. Tatum when you did."

"I just hate that we were too late for Nancy," Tony said sadly.

"If only I had figured it out sooner," Lacy whispered. "All the pieces of the puzzle were right there – I just couldn't see it."

"No one blames you, Lacy!" Margaret interjected. "Dr. Tatum was very sly and had Dr. Maddox doing his dirty work. She didn't have an idea what was going on, and she worked with him every day! What is going to happen to her now?"

"She was given immunity after she agreed to testify against him," Tony replied. "She'll likely be given probation – his trial will be in a few months, but I'm sure he's going away for a very long time. And there is still an investigation going on regarding the Namakuras. I imagine that they have broken all sorts of financial laws, but it will be difficult to prosecute since they are Japanese citizens."

Lacy added, "At least one good thing came of all this – Dr. Maddox's research had uncovered some interesting possibilities, and it has been turned over to a group of reputable gerontologists for further study. Hopefully an Alzheimer's breakthrough is on the way."

"That would be wonderful," Margaret replied, glancing at her father. "How is your mom doing, Lacy?"

"Oh, she's great. She loved partnering with me so much that she is now volunteering at the TV station as a receptionist. It's been fun getting to spend so much time with her. She keeps asking when she can go undercover again!"

"And you, Tony, we can't thank you enough for your help, too." Margaret added. "You are happy to be back on the street?"

"Oh, you bet! Internal Affairs took *forever* to clear me to go back on patrol, but it's where my heart is, mostly........." he said slyly as he gave Lacy a wink. She found herself blushing a bit, but reached out her hand and put it in his. They had been spending a lot of time together lately, which made both of them very happy.

"No more secrets!" Theodore said happily, and everyone raised their glass in a toast.

"No more secrets, dad." Margaret said softly as she kissed his cheek.